The Knight
in
Rusty Armor

Robert Fisher

MELVIN POWERS
WILSHIRE BOOK COMPANY

To my dear friends Dr. Gianni Boni, Sandra Dunn, and Dr. Robert Sharp, who taught me what I didn't know and awakened me to what I did know.

Published by Wilshire Book Company
22647 Ventura Blvd. #314, Woodland Hills, California 91364

www.mpowers.com

Library of Congress Control Number 86-51562
ISBN 0-87980-421-1
Printed in the United States of America

For information regarding quantity discounts for bulk purchases,
email sales@mpowers.com

Contents

CHAPTER ONE

The Knight's Dilemma

A long time ago in a land far away, there lived a knight who thought of himself as good, kind, and loving. He did all the things that good, kind, and loving knights do. He fought foes who were bad, mean, and hateful. He slew dragons and rescued fair damsels in distress. When the knight business was slow, he had the annoying habit of rescuing damsels even if they didn't need to be rescued. Although many ladies were grateful to him, just as many were furious with him. This he accepted philosophically. After all, one can't please everybody.

This knight was famous for his armor. It reflected such bright rays of light that villagers were convinced they could see the sun rise in the west or set in the east whenever the knight rode off to battle—which he did quite frequently. At the mere mention of a crusade, he would eagerly don his shining armor, mount his horse, and ride off in any direction. So eager was he, in fact, that sometimes he would ride off in several directions at once, which was no easy feat.

For years this knight strove to be the number one knight in all the kingdom. There was always another battle to be won, dragon to be slain, or damsel to be rescued.

The knight had a faithful and somewhat tolerant wife, Juliet, who wrote beautiful poetry, said clever things, and had a penchant for wine. He also had a golden-haired young son, Christopher, who he hoped would grow up to be a courageous knight.

Juliet and Christopher saw little of the knight because whenever he was not off fighting battles, slaying dragons, and rescuing damsels, he was busy trying on his armor and admiring its brilliance. As time went on, the knight became so enamored of his armor that he began wearing it to dinner and often to bed. Eventually he didn't bother to take it off at all. His family began to forget how he looked without it.

Occasionally Christopher would ask his mother what his father looked like underneath his armor. Juliet would lead the boy to the fireplace and point to a portrait of the knight above it. "There's your father," she would say with a sigh.

One afternoon while contemplating the portrait, Christopher said to his mother, "I wish I could see Father in person."

"Well, you can't have everything!" snapped Juliet. She was growing impatient and frustrated at having only a painting to remind her of her husband's face, and the constant clanking of armor at night had left her exhausted from lack of sleep.

Whenever the knight was home and not completely preoccupied with his armor, he was usually delivering rambling monologues on his exploits. Juliet and Christopher were seldom able to get a word in edgewise. If they did, the knight shut them out, either by closing his visor or by abruptly closing his eyes and going to sleep.

One day Juliet confronted her husband. "I think you love your armor more than you love me."

"That's not true," said the knight. His armor clanked loudly as he gestured with his arms. "Didn't I love you enough to rescue you from that dragon and set you up in this classy castle with wall-to-wall stones?"

"What you loved," corrected Juliet, peering through his visor so that she could see his eyes, "was the *idea* of rescuing me. You really didn't love me then, and you really don't love me now."

"I *do* love you," insisted the knight, hugging her clumsily in his cold, stiff armor and nearly breaking her ribs.

"Then take off that armor so I can see who you really are!" she demanded.

"I *can't* take it off. I have to be ready to mount my horse and ride off in any direction," explained the knight.

"If you don't take off that armor, I'm taking Christopher, getting on *my* horse, and riding out of your life."

This was a real blow to the knight. He didn't want Juliet to leave. He did love his wife and his son and his classy castle, but he also loved his armor because it showed everyone who he was—a good, kind, and loving knight. Why couldn't Juliet see that he was all of these things?

In turmoil the knight clanked off to his study. He thought and thought. Finally he came to a decision. Continuing to wear the armor wasn't worth losing Juliet and Christopher.

Reluctantly he reached up to remove his helmet. It didn't budge! He gave it a tug. It held fast. Dismayed, he tried lifting the visor but, alas, that was stuck too. He pulled on the visor again and again, to no avail.

The knight paced back and forth in great agitation. How could this have happened? He could understand why the helmet was stuck since he had not removed it for years, but the visor was another matter. He had opened it regularly to eat and drink. Why, he had lifted it just that morning to enjoy his breakfast of scrambled eggs and suckling pig.

Suddenly the knight had an idea. Without telling his family where he was going, he hurried to the blacksmith's shop in the castle courtyard. When he arrived, the smith was shaping a horseshoe with his bare hands.

"Smith," announced the knight, "I have a problem."

"You *are* a problem, sire," quipped the smith with his usual tact.

The knight, who normally enjoyed bantering, glowered. "I'm in no mood for your wisecracks right now," he bellowed. "I'm stuck in this armor." He stamped his steel-clad foot, accidentally bringing it down on the smith's big toe.

The smith let out a howl and, momentarily forgetting the knight was his master, dealt him a smashing blow to the helmet with the horseshoe. The knight felt only a twinge of discomfort. The helmet didn't budge.

"Do that again," ordered the knight, unaware that the smith had obliged him out of anger and pain.

"With pleasure," the smith agreed, grabbing a nearby hammer. Swinging it with vengeance, he brought it down squarely on the knight's helmet. It didn't even make a dent.

The knight was distraught. The smith was by far the strongest man in the kingdom. If he couldn't shuck the knight out of his armor, who could?

Being a kind man, except when his big toe was crushed, the smith sensed the knight's panic and grew sympathetic. "You have a tough plight, Knight, but don't give up. Come back tomorrow after I'm rested. You caught me at the end of a hard day."

"Very well," the knight said, turning to leave.

Dinnertime that evening was awkward. Juliet became increasingly annoyed as she pushed forkfuls of mashed food through the holes in the knight's visor. Partway through the meal, the knight told Juliet that the blacksmith had tried to split open the armor but had failed.

Juliet stopped. She picked up the half-full plate of pigeon stew. "I don't believe you, you clanking clod!" she shouted, smashing the plate over his helmet.

The knight felt nothing. Only when gravy began dripping down past the eyeholes in his visor did he realize that he had been hit on the head. He had barely felt the impact of the smith's hammer that afternoon either. In fact, now that he thought about it, his armor kept him from feeling much of anything, and he had worn it for so long that he had forgotten how things felt without it.

The knight was upset that Juliet didn't believe he was serious about trying to get his armor off. He *was* serious. He and the smith kept at it for many more days but without success. Each day the knight grew more despondent and Juliet grew colder.

Finally the knight had to admit that the smith's efforts were useless. "Strongest man in the kingdom indeed! You can't even break open this steel junkyard!" the knight yelled at him in frustration.

When the knight returned home, Juliet shrieked, "Your son has nothing but a portrait for a father, and I'm tired of talking to a visor. I'm never pushing food through the holes of that wretched thing again. I've mashed my very last mutton chop!"

"It's not *my* fault I got stuck in this armor," the knight whined. "I *had* to wear it so I would always be ready for battle. How else could I get nice castles and horses for you and Christopher?"

"You didn't do it for *us*," argued Juliet. "You did it for *yourself*!"

The knight was sick at heart that his wife didn't seem to love him anymore. And he feared that if he didn't get his armor off soon, Juliet and Christopher really would leave. He *had* to get the armor off, but he didn't know how.

He dismissed one idea after another as being unlikely to work. Some of the plans were downright dangerous. He knew that any knight who would even think of melting his armor off with a torch, freezing it off by jumping into an icy moat, or blasting it off with a cannon was badly in need of help. Unable to find it in his own kingdom, the knight decided to search in other lands. *Somewhere there must be someone who knows how to get this armor off,* he thought.

Of course he would miss Juliet and Christopher and his classy castle. And he was afraid that in his absence Juliet might find love with another knight, one willing to remove his armor at bedtime and be more of a father to Christopher. Nevertheless, he felt he had no choice. He had to go.

Early one morning he got onto his horse and rode away. He didn't dare look back for fear he might change his mind. On his way out of the province, the knight stopped to say good-bye to the king, who had been very good to him. The king lived in a grand castle atop a hill in the high-rent district. As the knight rode across the drawbridge and into the courtyard, he saw the court jester sitting cross-legged, playing a reed flute.

The jester was called Gladbag because he always carried a beautiful rainbow-colored bag filled with all sorts of things that made people laugh. There were strange cards that he used to tell people's fortunes, brightly colored beads that he made appear and disappear, and funny little puppets that he used to insult his audiences.

"Greetings, Gladbag," said the knight. "I came to say farewell to the king."

The jester looked up.

"The king has up and gone away.

To you there's nothing he can say."

"Where has he gone?" asked the knight.

"He's taken off on a new crusade.

If you wait for him, you'll be delayed."

The knight was disappointed that he had missed

the king and perturbed that he couldn't join him on the crusade. "Oh," he sighed. "I could starve to death in this armor by the time the king returns. I might never see him again." He felt like slumping in his saddle, but his armor wouldn't let him.

"Well, aren't you a silly sight?

All your might can't solve your plight."

"I'm in no mood for your insulting rhymes," barked the knight. "Can't you take someone's problem seriously for once?"

In a clear, lyrical voice, Gladbag sang:

"Problems never set me a-rockin'.

They're opportunities a-knockin'."

"You'd sing a different tune if *you* were the one stuck in here," growled the knight.

Gladbag retorted:

"We're all stuck in armor of a kind.

Yours is merely easier to find."

"I don't have time to stay and listen to this nonsense. I have to find a way to get out of this armor." With that, the knight kneed his mount and began trotting away, but Gladbag called after him:

"There is one who can help you, Knight,

to bring the real you into sight."

The knight pulled his horse to a stop. Excitedly, he turned back to Gladbag. "You know someone who can get me out of this armor? Who is it?"

"Merlin the Magician you must see.

Then you'll discover how to be free."

"Merlin? The only Merlin I've ever heard of is the great and wise teacher of King Arthur."

"Yes, yes, that's his claim to fame.

This Merlin I know is one and the same."

"But it can't be!" exclaimed the knight. "Merlin and Arthur lived long ago."

"It's true, yet he's alive and well.

In yonder woods the sage doth dwell."

"But the woods are so big," said the knight. "How will I find him?"

"One never knows be it days, weeks, or years.

When the pupil is ready, the teacher appears."

"Well, I'm not going to wait for Merlin to show up. I'm going to look for *him,*" the knight announced firmly. He reached down and shook Gladbag's hand in gratitude, nearly crushing the jester's fingers in his gauntlet.

Gladbag yelped. The knight quickly released his hand. "Oh, sorry."

The jester rubbed his bruised fingers.

"When the armor's gone from you,

you'll feel the pain of others too."

"I'm off!" boomed the knight, paying no mind to the remark. He wheeled his horse around and, with new hope in his heart, galloped away to find Merlin.

CHAPTER TWO

In Merlin's Woods

*I*t was no easy task to find the wizard. The woods were huge and seemingly endless. The poor knight rode on, day after day, night after night, becoming weaker and weaker.

As he continued, the knight realized there were many things he didn't know. He had always thought of himself as very smart, but right now he didn't feel smart at all trying to survive in the woods.

Reluctantly he admitted to himself that he didn't even know poisonous berries from edible ones. This made eating a game of Russian roulette. Drinking was no less hazardous. The knight tried sticking his head into a stream, but his helmet filled up with water. Twice he almost drowned. As if that wasn't bad enough, he had been lost ever since he entered the woods. He couldn't tell north from south or east from west. Fortunately his horse could.

After searching and searching in vain, the knight was quite discouraged. He still hadn't found Merlin even though he had traveled many leagues. What made him feel worse was the fact that he didn't even know how far a league was.

One morning he awoke feeling weaker than usual and a little peculiar. That was the morning he found Merlin. The knight recognized the magician at once. He was sitting under a tree, clothed in a long white robe. Animals of the forest were gathered around him, and birds were perched on his shoulders and arms.

The knight shook his head glumly, his helmet squeaking. *How could all these animals find Merlin so easily when it was so hard for me?*

Wearily he climbed down from his horse. "I've been looking for you. I've been lost for months."

"You've been lost all your life," corrected Merlin, snapping off a piece of carrot and sharing it with the nearest rabbit.

The knight stiffened. "I didn't come all this way to be insulted."

"Perhaps you have always taken the truth to be an insult," said Merlin, sharing the rest of the carrot with some of the other animals.

The knight didn't care for this remark either, but he was too weak from hunger and thirst to climb back onto his horse and ride away. He dropped his metal-encased body onto the grass and leaned back against a tree with a clank.

Merlin looked at him compassionately. "You are most fortunate. You are too weak to run."

"What's that supposed to mean?" snapped the knight.

Merlin smiled. "A person cannot run and also learn. He must stay in one place for a while."

The knight raised his hand and jabbed a gloved finger at the ground. "I'm going to stay here only long enough to learn how to get out of this armor."

"Once you learn that, you will never again have to climb on your horse and ride off in all directions."

The knight was too tired to question this. Somehow he felt comforted and fell promptly asleep.

When the knight awoke, Merlin and the animals were gathered around him. He tried to sit up but was too weak. Merlin held out a silver cup with a strange-colored liquid in it. "Here. Drink this."

"What is it?" asked the knight, eyeing the cup suspiciously.

"You are so afraid," said Merlin. "Of course, that is why you put on the armor in the first place."

The knight didn't deny this, for he was too thirsty. "All right, I'll drink it. Pour it into my visor."

"I will not," Merlin replied. "It is too precious to waste." He plucked a reed, put one end in the cup, and slipped the other through one of the holes in the knight's visor.

"This is a great idea!" blurted the knight, taking the cup.

"I call it a straw," Merlin said simply.

"Why?"

"Why not?"

The knight shrugged. He sipped the liquid through the reed. The first sips tasted bitter, the later ones more pleasant, and the last swallows quite delicious. Grateful, the knight handed the cup back to Merlin. "You should put that stuff on the market. You could sell flagons of it."

Merlin smiled.

"What is it?" asked the knight.

"Life," Merlin replied.

"Life?"

"Yes. Did the liquid not at first seem bitter? Then, as you tasted more of it, was it not pleasant?"

The knight nodded. "Yes, and the last swallows were quite delicious."

"That was when you began to accept what you were drinking."

"Are you saying that life is good when you accept it?"

"Is it not?" countered Merlin, raising an eyebrow in amusement.

"Do you really expect me to accept all this heavy armor?"

"Ah," said Merlin, "you were not born with that armor. You put it on yourself. Have you ever asked why?"

"Why not?" retorted the knight, irritated. His head

was beginning to hurt. He wasn't used to thinking in this manner.

"You will be able to think more clearly once you regain your strength," Merlin explained.

With that, the magician clapped his hands twice, and the squirrels, holding nuts in their little mouths, lined up in front of the knight. Each squirrel climbed up onto the knight's shoulder, cracked open and chewed a nut, then pushed the pieces through the knight's visor. The rabbits did the same with carrots, and the deer crushed roots and berries for the knight to eat. This method of feeding would never be endorsed by the health department, but what else could a knight who was stuck in his armor in the woods possibly do?

The animals fed the knight regularly, and Merlin gave him large cups of Life to drink through the straw. The knight grew stronger, and he began to feel more hopeful.

Each day he asked Merlin the same question: "When will I get out of this armor?" And each day Merlin replied, "Patience! You have been wearing that armor for a long time. You cannot get out of it just like that."

One night the animals and the knight were listening to the magician strum the latest troubadour hits on his lute. After Merlin had finished playing "Hark Ye the Days of Old, When Knights Were Bold and

Maidens Were Cold," the knight asked a question long on his mind. "Were you really the teacher of King Arthur?"

The magician's face lit up. "Yes, I taught Arthur."

"But how can you still be alive? He lived eons ago!"

"Past, present, and future are all one when you are connected to the Source," Merlin said.

"What is the Source?"

"It is the mysterious, invisible power that is the origin of all."

The knight was puzzled. "I don't understand."

"That is because you are trying to understand with your mind, but your mind is limited."

Merlin's words stung. "I have a very good mind," said the knight, offended.

"And a clever one," added Merlin. "It trapped you in all that armor."

The knight could not refute this. Then he remembered something Merlin had said to him when he first arrived. "You said I put on this armor because I was afraid."

"Is that not true?"

"No, I wear it for protection when I go into battle."

"So you put it on because you were afraid you would be seriously hurt or killed," Merlin clarified.

"Isn't everybody?"

The magician shook his head. "Whoever said you had to go into battle?"

"I had to prove I was a good, kind, and loving knight."

"If you really *were* good, kind, and loving, why did you have to prove it?"

The knight escaped thinking about this in his usual manner of escaping things—he drifted off to sleep.

The following morning he awoke with an odd thought: *Is it possible that I'm not good, kind, and loving?* He asked Merlin.

"What do *you* think?" Merlin replied.

"Why do you always answer a question with another question?"

"And why do you always seek the answers to your questions from others?"

The knight stomped off angrily, cursing Merlin under his breath. "That Merlin!" he muttered. "Sometimes he really gets under my armor!"

With a thud the knight dropped his burdened body under a tree to contemplate the magician's questions. *What do I think?* "Could it be," he said aloud to no one in particular, "that I'm *not* good, kind, and loving?"

"Could be," a little voice piped up. "Otherwise, why are you sitting on my tail?"

"Huh?" The knight was startled. He peered down and saw a squirrel sitting beside him. That is, most of the squirrel. Her tail was hidden from view.

"Oh, excuse me!" he said, shifting his weight so the little creature could reclaim her tail. "I hope I didn't hurt you. I can't see very well with this visor in my way."

"I don't doubt that," replied the squirrel without resentment. "That's why you have to keep apologizing to people for hurting them."

The knight's demeanor quickly changed to annoyance. "The only thing that irritates me more than a smart-aleck magician is a smart-aleck squirrel. I don't have to stay here and talk to you."

He struggled to get to his feet. Suddenly he blurted out in amazement, "Hey . . . you and I are talking!"

"A tribute to my good nature," said the squirrel, "considering that you sat on my tail."

"But animals can't talk!"

"Sure we can. It's just that people don't listen."

The knight shook his head in bewilderment. "You've talked to me before?"

"Certainly. Every time I cracked a nut and pushed it through your visor."

"How can I hear you now when I couldn't hear you then?"

"I admire an inquiring mind," mused the squirrel, "but don't you ever accept anything the way it is—just because it *is*."

"You're answering my questions with questions. You've been around Merlin too long."

"And you haven't been around him long enough." The squirrel flicked her tail at the knight and scampered up the tree.

The knight called after her. "Wait! What's your name?"

"Squirrel," she called back. Then she vanished into the topmost branches.

Dazed, the knight shook his head, his helmet squeaking. Had he imagined all this? He began to worry he was losing his mind. At that moment, he saw Merlin approaching. "Merlin, I *have* to get out of here. I've started talking to squirrels!"

Merlin raised his hands and clasped them together. "Splendid."

The knight was perplexed. "What do you mean, splendid?"

"Just that. You are becoming sensitive enough to feel the vibrations of others."

The knight was obviously confused, so Merlin continued explaining. "You did not talk to the squirrel in words, but you felt her vibrations, and you translated those vibrations into words." He patted the night on the shoulder. "I am looking forward to the day when you start talking to flowers."

The knight shrugged him off angrily. "That'll be the day you plant them on my grave. I have to get out of these woods!"

"Where will you go?"

"Back to Juliet and Christopher. They've been alone for too long. I have to get back and take care of them."

"How can you take care of *them* when you cannot even take care of *yourself*?" Merlin asked.

"But I miss them," whined the knight. "I want to go back to them in the worst way."

"And that is exactly how you will go back if you stay in your armor," cautioned Merlin.

The knight looked at Merlin pleadingly. "I don't want to wait until I get the armor off. I want to go back now and be a good, kind, and loving husband to Juliet and a good father to Christopher."

Merlin nodded in understanding. He told the knight that going back to give of himself was a lovely gift. "However, a gift, to be a gift, has to be accepted. Otherwise it lies like a burden between people."

"You mean they may not want me back?" asked the knight fearfully. "Surely they would give me another chance. After all, I *am* one of the top knights in the kingdom."

"Perhaps that armor is thicker than it appears," Merlin said gently.

The knight thought about this. He remembered Juliet's endless complaints about his going off to battle so often, about the attention he showered on his armor, and about his closed visor and his habit of abruptly going to sleep to shut her out. "Maybe Juliet *wouldn't* want me back, but certainly Christopher would," he said aloud.

"Why not send Christopher a note and ask him?"

The knight agreed this was a good idea, but how would he get the note to his son? Merlin pointed to the pigeon sitting on his shoulder. "Rebecca will take it."

"She doesn't know where I live. She's only a stupid bird," said the knight with disdain.

"I can tell north from south and east from west," snapped Rebecca, "which is more than I can say for you."

The knight quickly apologized. He was thoroughly shaken. Not only had he talked to both a pigeon and a squirrel, but he had gotten both of them angry at him in the same day. Bighearted bird that she was, Rebecca accepted the knight's apology and flew off with his hastily written note to Christopher in her beak.

"Don't coo at any strange pigeons or you'll drop my note," the knight called after her.

Rebecca ignored his thoughtless remark. The knight had much to learn.

A week passed and Rebecca had not returned. The knight grew more and more anxious, fearing she might have fallen prey to one of the hunting falcons he and other knights had trained. He winced, wondering how he could have participated in such a foul sport. Then he winced again at his awful pun.

When Merlin finished playing his lute and singing "You'll Have a Long, Cold Winter if You Have a Short, Cold Heart," the knight expressed his concern. Merlin reassured him by making up a happy little verse:

"The smartest pigeon who ever flew

will never wind up in someone's stew."

All at once a great chattering arose from the animals. They were all looking skyward. Merlin and the knight looked up. High above them, circling for a landing, was Rebecca. The knight struggled to his feet just as Rebecca swooped down onto Merlin's shoulder. The magician took the note from her beak and glanced at it. Gravely he told the knight it was from Christopher.

"Let me see!" said the knight, grabbing the note eagerly. His jaw dropped with a clank as he stared at the note in disbelief. "It's blank!" he exclaimed. "What does that mean?"

"It means," said Merlin softly, "that your son does not know enough about you to give you an answer."

Stunned, the knight stood speechless for a moment. Then he groaned and sank to the ground. He tried to choke back the tears, for knights in shining armor never cry. But his grief soon overwhelmed him.

Finally, exhausted and half-drowned from the tears in his helmet, he fell asleep.

CHAPTER THREE

The Path of Truth

W hen the knight awoke, Merlin was sitting beside him. "I'm sorry I acted so unknightly," the knight said. He looked down at his tear-soaked beard, adding in disgust, "My beard got all soggy."

"Do not apologize," said Merlin. "You have just taken the first step toward getting out of your armor."

"What do you mean?"

"You will see," replied the magician. He stood up. "It is time for you to go."

This disturbed the knight. He had come to enjoy living in the woods with Merlin and the animals. It seemed he had no place to go anyway. Juliet and Christopher apparently didn't want him to come home. True, he could get back into the knight business and go on some crusades. He had a good reputation in battle and there were several kings who would be happy to have him, but fighting no longer seemed to have any purpose.

Merlin reminded the knight of his new purpose: to get rid of his armor.

"Why bother?" the knight asked morosely. "It doesn't matter to Juliet and Christopher whether I get my armor off or not."

"Do it for yourself," said Merlin. "Being trapped in all that steel has caused you much difficulty, and things will only get worse as time goes on. You could even die by catching pneumonia from a soggy beard."

The knight reflected on the magician's words. "I suppose my armor *has* become a nuisance. I'm tired of lugging it around, and I'm fed up with eating mushy food. Come to think of it, I can't even scratch my back when it itches."

"And how long has it been since you have felt the warmth of a kiss, smelled the sweet fragrance of a flower, or heard a beautiful melody without your armor getting in the way?"

"I can hardly remember," the knight muttered sadly. "You're right, Merlin. I have to get this armor off for *myself.*"

"You cannot continue living and thinking as you have in the past. That is how you got stuck in your steel prison in the first place."

"But how am I ever going to change all that?"

"It is not as difficult as it may seem," Merlin explained. He helped the knight stand up, then led him to a path. "This was the path you followed to get into these woods."

"I didn't follow any path. I was lost for months!"

"People are often unaware of the path they are on," stated Merlin.

"You mean this path was here, but I couldn't see it?"

"Yes, and you can go back that way if you want to, but it leads to dishonesty, greed, hatred, jealousy, fear, and ignorance."

The knight was indignant. "Are you saying that I'm all those things?"

"At times, you are some of those things," Merlin replied. He pointed to another path. It was narrower and very steep.

"That looks like a tough climb," observed the knight.

Merlin nodded in agreement. "That," he said, "is the Path of Truth. It grows steeper as it approaches the summit of a mountain far in the distance."

The knight looked at the trail without enthusiasm. "I'm not sure it's worth it. What will I have when I get to the top?"

"It is what you *won't* have," corrected Merlin. "Your armor."

The knight pondered this. If he returned to the path he had traveled before, there would be no hope of removing his armor and he would probably die of loneliness and fatigue. The only way to get the armor off, it seemed, was to follow the Path of Truth, but then he might lose his life on the treacherous mountainside.

He looked at the difficult path ahead. Then he looked down at the steel covering his body.

"OK," he said with resignation. "I'll try the Path of Truth."

Merlin smiled slightly. "Your decision to travel an unknown trail while encumbered with heavy armor takes great courage."

The knight knew he had better start right away before he changed his mind. "I'll get my trusty horse."

"Oh no," said Merlin, shaking his head. "The path has areas too narrow for a horse to pass. You will have to go on foot."

Aghast, the knight plunked himself down on a rock with a clang. "I think I'd rather die of pneumonia from a soggy beard," he said, his courage waning rapidly.

"You will not have to travel alone," Merlin told him. "Squirrel will accompany you."

"What do you expect me to do, ride squirrel-back?" asked the knight, dreading the thought of making the arduous journey with a smart-talking squirrel.

"You might not be able to ride me," said Squirrel, "but you'll need me to help you eat. Who else is going to chew nuts for you and push them through your visor?"

Rebecca flew over from a nearby tree and landed on the knight's shoulder. "I'll go with you too. I've been to the top of the mountain and I know the way."

The willingness of the two animals to help restored the knight's courage.

Well, isn't this something, he thought. *One of the top knights in the kingdom getting encouragement from a squirrel and a bird!* He struggled to his feet, signaling to Merlin that he was ready to begin his journey.

As they walked toward the Path of Truth, the magician took an exquisite golden key from his neck and gave it to the knight. "This key will open the doors to three castles that will block your path—"

"I know!" the knight interrupted. "There will be a princess inside each castle and I'll slay the dragon guarding her and rescue—"

"Enough!" Merlin said sternly. "There will be no princesses in any of these castles. Even if there were, you are in no shape to be rescuing anyone. You must learn to save yourself first."

Reprimanded, the knight grew quiet while Merlin continued. "The first castle is named Silence; the second, Knowledge; and the third, Will and Daring. Once you enter each of them, you will find your way out only after you have learned what you are there to learn."

This didn't sound nearly as much fun as rescuing princesses. Besides, at the moment, castle tours really didn't appeal to the knight. "Why can't I just go around them?" he asked.

"If you do, you'll stray from the path and you are

certain to get lost. The only way you can get to the top of the mountain is to go through those castles," Merlin said firmly.

The knight sighed deeply as he gazed up the steep, narrow trail. It disappeared between tall trees that jutted up toward some low-hanging clouds. He sensed this journey was going to be much more difficult than any of his crusades.

Merlin knew what the knight was thinking. "Yes, there is a different battle to be fought on the Path of Truth. The fight will be learning to love yourself."

"How will I do that?"

"It will begin with learning to know yourself." Merlin gestured at the knight's weapon. "This battle cannot be won with your sword. You must leave it here."

The magician gazed at the knight for a moment as he drew his sword and placed it at Merlin's feet. Then he added, "If you encounter anything you cannot handle, just call me and I will come."

"You mean you can appear anywhere?"

"Any self-respecting magician can do that," Merlin said matter-of-factly. Then he disappeared.

The knight was astounded. "Why . . . why, he vanished!"

Squirrel nodded. "He really hams it up sometimes."

"You're going to waste all your energy talking," Rebecca scolded. "Let's get going."

The knight's helmet squeaked as he shook his head in assent.

They started out with Squirrel in the lead, followed by the knight with Rebecca on his shoulder. From time to time Rebecca flew ahead and returned to report what lay in store.

After a few hours the knight collapsed, exhausted and sore. He wasn't used to traveling without his horse. Since it was almost dark anyway, Rebecca and Squirrel decided they might as well stop for the night.

Rebecca flitted among the bushes and gathered some berries, which she pushed through the holes in the knight's visor. Squirrel went to a nearby brook and filled some walnut shells with water, which the knight drank through the straw that Merlin had given him. Too tired to stay awake for the nuts Squirrel was preparing, the knight fell asleep.

He was awakened the next morning by the sun shining in his eyes. Unaccustomed to the glare, he squinted. His visor had never before allowed in so much light. As he was trying to figure out the reason for this phenomenon, Squirrel and Rebecca were staring at him, chattering and cooing excitedly.

Pushing himself to a sitting position, he suddenly realized that he could see more than he could the day before. What's more, he could feel the cool air against his face. His visor had broken off! *How did that happen?* he wondered.

Squirrel answered his unspoken question. "It rusted and fell off."

"But how?"

"From the tears you cried after you saw your son's blank letter," Rebecca said jubilantly.

The knight stopped to think. The sorrow he had felt was so deep that his armor could not protect him from it. Quite the contrary, his tears had actually started to break down the steel surrounding him.

"That's it!" he shouted with glee. "Tears from real feelings will release me from my armor!"

He got to his feet faster than he had in years. "Squirrel! Rebecca! Forsooth!" he cried. "Let's hit the Path of Truth!"

Rebecca and Squirrel were so overjoyed that neither mentioned this was a terrible rhyme.

The three of them continued up the mountain. It was an especially fine day for the knight. With his visor gone, he now noticed tiny sunlit particles in the air as they filtered through the branches of the trees. Looking closely at the faces of some robins, he saw that they didn't all look alike. He mentioned this to Rebecca, who hopped up and down, cooing merrily. "You're starting to see the differences in other forms of life because you're starting to see the differences within yourself."

The knight tried to figure out exactly what Rebecca meant. But he was too proud to ask, for he still thought a knight should be smarter than a pigeon.

Just then Squirrel, who had gone scouting ahead, came scampering back. "The Castle of Silence is just over the next rise."

Excited at the thought of seeing the first castle, the knight clanked forward even faster. He reached the top of the hill, quite out of breath. Sure enough, a castle loomed ahead, completely blocking the path. The knight sighed with disappointment. He had expected a very fancy structure. Instead, the Castle of Silence looked just like any other tract castle.

Rebecca laughed. "When you learn to *accept* instead of *expect,* you'll have fewer disappointments."

The knight nodded at the wisdom of this. "I've spent most of my life being disappointed. I remember lying in my crib thinking I was the most beautiful baby in the whole world. Then my nurse looked down at me and said, 'You have a face only a mother could love.' I wound up being disappointed in myself for being ugly instead of beautiful, and I was disappointed in the nurse for being so impolite."

"If you had truly accepted yourself as beautiful, it wouldn't have mattered what she said. You wouldn't have been disappointed," Squirrel explained.

This made sense to the knight. "I'm beginning to think animals are smarter than people."

"The fact that you can say that makes you as smart as we are," Squirrel said, twitching her tail.

"I don't think it has anything to do with being smart," commented Rebecca. "Animals *accept* and humans *expect*. You'll never hear a rabbit say, 'I expect the sun to come out this morning so I can go down to the lake and play.' If the sun doesn't come out, it won't ruin the rabbit's whole day. He's happy just being a rabbit."

The knight mulled this over. He couldn't recall many people who were happy just being people.

As they approached the castle, it appeared larger and larger. When they reached the door, the knight took the golden key from around his neck and inserted it into the lock. As he turned the key, Rebecca whispered, "We're not going in with you."

The knight, who was learning to love and trust the two animals, was disappointed. He almost said so but caught himself. He was expecting again.

The animals knew the knight was reluctant to step into the castle. "We can show you the door," said Squirrel, "but you have to walk through it alone."

Rebecca said cheerily, "We'll meet you on the other side."

Nodding, the knight took a deep breath and opened the door wide.

CHAPTER FOUR

The Castle of Silence

*T*he knight cautiously poked his head through the doorway of the castle. His knees trembled slightly, causing his armor to make a low metallic rattle. Not wanting to look like a chicken to a pigeon and a squirrel, he pulled himself together and walked boldly inside, closing the door behind him. For a moment he wished he hadn't left his sword with Merlin, but the magician had promised there would be no dragons to slay, and the knight trusted him.

He walked into the huge anteroom of the castle and looked around. A fire blazed in an enormous stone fireplace, and three rugs lay on the floor. He sat down on the rug nearest the fire.

Soon the knight became aware of two things about this castle: First, there seemed to be no door leading out of the room. Second, there was an extraordinary, eerie silence. With a start, he realized the fire wasn't even crackling. The knight had thought of his own castle as quiet, especially whenever Juliet didn't speak to him for days at a time, but it was nothing like this.

The Castle of Silence is well named, he thought. Never in his life had he felt so alone.

Suddenly he heard a familiar voice behind him. "Hello, Knight."

The knight whirled and was astonished to see the king approaching him from a far corner of the room.

"King!" he gasped, struggling to his feet. "I didn't even see you. What are you doing here?"

"The same thing you are, Knight—looking for the door."

The knight looked around again. "I don't see any door."

"One really can't see until one understands," said the king. "When you understand what's in this room, you'll be able to see the door to the next."

"I certainly hope so, King. I'm surprised to see you here. I heard you were on a crusade."

"That's what I say whenever I travel the Path of Truth," the king explained. "It's easier for my subjects to understand."

The knight looked puzzled.

"Everybody understands crusades," the king went on, "but very few understand truth."

"Yes," agreed the knight. "I wouldn't be on this path myself if I wasn't trapped in this armor."

"Most of us are trapped inside our armor."

"What do you mean?"

"We put up barriers to protect who we think we

are. Then one day we get stuck behind the barriers and we can't get out."

"I never thought of you as being stuck, King. You're so wise."

The king laughed ruefully. "I have enough wisdom to know when I'm stuck and to return here so I can learn more about myself."

The knight was greatly encouraged, thinking perhaps the king could show him the way. "Say," he began, his face brightening, "could we go through the castle together? That way we wouldn't be so lonely."

The king shook his head. "I once tried that. It's true that my companions and I weren't lonely because we talked constantly, but when one talks it's impossible to see the door out of this room."

"Maybe we could just walk and be quiet together," suggested the knight. He wasn't looking forward to wandering around the Castle of Silence by himself.

The king shook his head again, harder this time. "No, I tried that too. It made the emptiness less painful, but I still couldn't see the door out of this room."

"But if you weren't talking—"

"Being quiet is more than not talking," said the king. "I discovered that when I was with someone, I showed only my best image. I wouldn't let down my barriers and allow either myself or the other person to see what I was trying to hide."

The knight frowned. "I don't get it."

"You will," replied the king, "when you have been here long enough. One must be alone to drop one's armor."

Dismayed, the knight exclaimed, "I don't want to stay here by myself!" He stamped his foot emphatically, inadvertently bringing it down on the king's big toe.

The king yelled in pain and hopped around, holding his throbbing foot.

The knight was horrified. First the smith, now the king. "Sorry, sire," the knight said apologetically.

The king rubbed his toe. "Oh well. That armor hurts you more than it hurts me." Then, standing tall, he looked knowingly at the knight. "I understand that you don't want to stay in this castle by yourself. Neither did I when I first began coming here, but now I realize that what one must do here, one must do alone." With that, he limped across the room, adding, "I must be on my way now."

The knight was perplexed. "Where are you going? The door is over here."

"That door is only an entrance. The door to the next room is on the far wall. I finally saw it just now."

"What do you mean you finally saw it? Didn't you remember where it was from the other times you were here?" asked the knight, wondering why the king would bother to keep coming back.

"One never finishes traveling the Path of Truth.

36

Each time I come here, I find new doors as I under-stand more and more." The king waved. "Be good to yourself, my friend."

"Wait! Please!" called the knight.

The king looked back at him compassionately. "Yes?"

Knowing he couldn't shake the king's resolve, the knight could only ask, "Is . . . is there any advice you can give me before you go?"

The king thought for a moment. "This is a new kind of crusade for you, dear Knight—one that requires more courage than all the other battles you've fought before. It will be your greatest victory if you can summon the strength to stay and do what you need to do here."

With that, he turned, reached out as if to open a door, and disappeared into the wall, leaving the knight staring disbelievingly after him. The knight hurried over to where the king had been, hoping to see the door as well. Finding what appeared to be only a solid wall, he began to pace around the room. All the knight could hear was the clanking of his armor echoing throughout the castle.

After a while he felt more depressed than he ever had in his life. To cheer himself up, he sang a couple of rousing battle songs: "I'll Be Down to Get You in a Crusade, Honey" and "Anywhere I Hang My Helmet Is Home." He sang them over and over again. As his voice grew tired, he stopped singing. The stillness became overwhelming, enveloping him in utter, devastating quiet. Only then could he frankly admit something he had never acknowledged before: He was afraid to be alone.

At that moment he saw a door in the far wall of the room. He crossed over to it, slowly pulled it open, and stepped through it into another room. This chamber appeared very much like the last, except it was somewhat smaller. It too was void of all sound.

Deciding to make himself comfortable, the knight settled down in front of the fire. To pass the time, he began talking aloud to himself. He said anything that came into his mind. He talked about what he was like as a little boy and how he was different from the other boys he knew. While they hunted quail and played Pin the Tail on the Boar, he stayed indoors and read. Since books were handwritten by the monks back then, they were few, and soon he had read them all. Then he began talking eagerly to anyone who passed his way. When there was no one to talk to, he talked to himself—just as he was doing now.

Unexpectedly the knight found himself saying that the reason he had talked so much all his life was to keep himself from feeling alone. He thought hard about this until the sound of his own voice broke the chilly silence. "I guess I've *always* been afraid to be alone."

As he spoke these words, another door became visible. The knight got up, opened the door, and stepped into the next room. It was smaller than the previous one, with a smaller fireplace and only two rugs. He sat down in front of the fire and continued thinking. Soon he realized that all his life he had wasted time talking about what he had done and what he was going to do. He had never enjoyed what was happening at the moment.

Yet another door appeared. It led to a room even smaller than the last, with a tiny fireplace and only one rug.

Encouraged by his progress, the knight did something he had never done before. He sat still in front of the fire and *listened* to the silence. It occurred to him that for most of his life, he really hadn't listened to anyone or anything. The rustle of the wind, the patter of the rain, and the sound of water running through a brook must have always been there, but he never actually *heard* them. Nor had he heard Juliet when she tried to tell him how she felt, especially when she was sad, because it reminded the knight that he was sad too. In fact, one of the reasons he had left on his armor all the time was that it muffled the sound of Juliet's sad voice. All he had to do was pull down his visor and he could shut her out completely.

Juliet must have felt very lonely talking to a man encased in steel — as lonely as he felt right now sitting in this tomblike room. His own pain and loneliness welled up inside him. Soon he felt Juliet's pain and loneliness too. *For years I forced her to live in a castle of silence,* he thought. He burst into tears.

The knight cried for so long that his tears spilled out and soaked the rug beneath him. The tears flowed into the fireplace and doused the fire. Indeed, the entire room was starting to flood, and the knight might have drowned if another door hadn't appeared in the wall just then.

Exhausted and emotionally spent, he waded to the door and pulled it open. The next room wasn't much bigger than the stall where he kept his horse. "I wonder why these rooms keep getting smaller," he asked himself aloud.

"Because you're closing in on yourself," a voice replied.

Startled, the knight looked around. He was alone—or so he thought. Who had spoken?

"*You* did," said the voice.

The voice seemed to come from within himself. *Could it be?* he wondered.

"Yes, it *could* be. I am the *real* you."

"But *I'm* the real me," protested the knight.

"Look at yourself," said the voice in disgust, "standing there half-starved in that hunk of junk, with a missing visor and soggy beard. If *you're* the real you, both of us are in trouble!"

"Now see here," the knight said indignantly, "I've lived all these years without hearing a word from you. Now that I do, the first thing you say is that you are the real me. Why haven't you spoken up before?"

"I've been around for years," continued the voice, "but this is the first time *you've* been quiet enough to hear me."

A sense of uneasiness came over the knight. "If you're the real *me*, then pray tell, who am *I*?" he said, worried.

The voice replied gently, changing its tone. "You can't expect to learn everything at once. Why don't you get some sleep."

"All right," said the knight. But before I do, I want to know what to call you."

"Call me? Why, I'm *you*."

"I can't call you *me*. It confuses me."

"OK. Call me Sam."

"Why Sam?"

"Why not?"

The knight rolled his eyes. "You must know Merlin," he murmured. His head was beginning to droop from lack of sleep. He lowered himself to the floor, closed his eyes, and fell into a deep, peaceful slumber.

When the knight awoke, he didn't know where he was. He was aware only of himself. The rest of the world seemed to have vanished. As he became more fully awake, he realized that Squirrel and Rebecca were sitting on his chest. "How did you get in here?" he asked.

Squirrel laughed. "We're not in *there*."

"You're out *here*," Rebecca cooed.

The knight opened his eyes wider and pushed himself up to a sitting position. He looked around in amazement. Sure enough, he was lying on the Path of Truth, just on the other side of the Castle of Silence.

"How did I get out of there?"

Rebecca answered, "The only way possible. You *thought* your way out."

"The last thing I remember," said the knight, "I was talking to—" He stopped himself. He wanted to tell Squirrel and Rebecca about Sam, but it wasn't easy to explain. Besides, he thought he might have imagined the whole thing. He had a lot to think about. The knight reached up to scratch his head. It took him a moment to realize that he was actually scratching his own scalp. He clasped both of his gauntleted hands to his head. His helmet was gone! As if for the first time, he touched his face and his long, scraggly beard in wonder.

"Squirrel! Rebecca!" he shouted with joy.

"We know," they said merrily in unison. "You must have cried again in the Castle of Silence."

"I did, but how could a whole helmet rust overnight?"

The animals laughed uproariously. Rebecca lay gasping and flapping on the ground. The knight thought she was going out of her bird. He demanded to know what was so funny.

Squirrel was the first to catch her breath. "You weren't in the castle just overnight, you know."

"Then for how long?"

"What if I told you that while you were in there I could have easily gathered more than five thousand nuts?"

"I would say *you're* nuts!" exclaimed the knight.

"You *were* in the castle for a long, long time," confirmed Rebecca, wiping a tear from her eye.

The knight's jaw dropped open in disbelief. He looked toward the sky and shouted, "Merlin, I must speak with you!"

As promised, the magician appeared immediately. He was naked except for his long beard, and he was dripping wet. Apparently the knight had caught him taking a bath.

"Oh, uh . . . suh-sorry about the intrusion," stammered the knight, averting his eyes. "But this is an emergency! I—"

Merlin held up his hand. "It is all right," he interrupted. "Magicians are often inconvenienced." He squeezed the water from his beard. "To answer your question, it is true. You *were* in the Castle of Silence for a very long time."

Merlin never failed to astound the knight. "How could you know I was going to ask you that?"

"Since I know myself, I know you. We are all part of one another."

The knight thought for a moment. "I'm beginning to understand. You mean I could feel Juliet's pain because I'm part of her?"

"Yes. That is why you could cry for her as well as for yourself. That was the first time you shed tears for another."

The knight told Merlin he felt proud. The magician smiled indulgently. "One does not have to feel proud of being human. It is as pointless as it would be for Rebecca to feel proud that she can fly. Rebecca was born with wings. You were born with a heart—and now you are using it, just as you were meant to do."

"You really know how to bring a fella down, Merlin."

"I did not mean to be hard on you. You are doing very well, or you never would have met Sam."

The knight felt relieved. "Then I really *did* hear him? It wasn't just my imagination?"

Merlin chuckled. "No, Sam is *real*—in fact, a more real you than the one you have been calling *I* all these years. You are not going crazy. You are starting to listen to your real self. That is why time passed so swiftly without your realizing it."

"I don't understand."

"You will by the time you go through the Castle of Knowledge."

Before the knight could ask any more questions, Merlin disappeared.

CHAPTER FIVE

The Castle of Knowledge

The knight, Squirrel, and Rebecca started out once more on the Path of Truth, headed toward the Castle of Knowledge. They stopped only twice that day, once to eat and once for the knight to shave off his scraggly beard and cut his long hair with the sharp edge of his gauntlet.

Afterward the knight looked and felt much better, and he was more free now than he had been before. With his helmet gone, he could eat nuts without Squirrel's help. Though he appreciated that lifesaving technique, he really didn't consider it gracious living. He could also feed himself the fruits and roots he had become accustomed to. Never again would he eat pigeon or any other fowl or meat, because he realized that in doing so he literally would be having friends for dinner.

Just before nightfall the trio trudged over a hill and saw the Castle of Knowledge in the distance. It was larger than the Castle of Silence, and its door was solid gold. This was the largest castle the knight had ever seen, even larger than the one the king had built for himself. The knight stared at the impressive structure and wondered who had designed it.

At that very moment the knight's thoughts were interrupted by Sam's voice. "The Castle of Knowledge was designed by the universe itself—the source of all knowledge."

The knight was surprised but pleased to hear from Sam again. "Glad you're back."

"Actually, I never left," Sam said. "Remember, I'm *you*."

"Please, I don't want to go through that again. How do you like me now that I've had a shave and a haircut?"

"It's the first time you ever profited from being clipped," Sam replied dryly.

The knight laughed. He liked Sam's sense of humor. If the Castle of Knowledge was anything like the Castle of Silence, he would be happy to have Sam along for company.

With Squirrel and Rebecca at his side, the knight crossed the drawbridge and stopped before the golden door. He took the key from around his neck and turned it in the lock. As he pushed the door open, he asked Rebecca and Squirrel if they were going to leave as they had before.

"No," Rebecca said. "Silence is for one; knowledge is for all."

The knight wondered how the word *pigeon* had come to mean an easy mark.

The three friends walked through the doorway and into a darkness so dense the knight couldn't even see his own hand. He groped around, looking for the customary torches by the castle door to light the way, but there weren't any. *A castle with a door of gold and no torches?* "Even cheap tract castles have torches," he grumbled.

Squirrel called out to him. The knight carefully felt his way to her and saw that she was pointing to a glowing inscription on the wall. It read:

KNOWLEDGE IS THE LIGHT BY WHICH
YOU SHALL FIND YOUR WAY.

I'd rather have a torch, thought the knight. *Whoever runs this castle sure is clever at cutting down on light bills.*

Sam spoke up. "It means that the more you know, the lighter it will get in here."

"Sam, I'll wager you're right!" exclaimed the knight. Just then a glimmer of light appeared around him.

Squirrel called out again to the knight. She had found another glowing inscription:

HAVE YOU MISTAKEN NEED FOR LOVE?

Still perturbed, the knight mumbled sarcastically,

"I suppose I have to figure out the answer before I get any more light."

"You're catching on quickly," came Sam's reply, to which the knight snorted, "I don't have time to play Twenty Questions. I want to find my way through this castle fast so I can get to the top of the mountain!"

"Maybe what you're supposed to learn here is that you have all the time in the world," suggested Rebecca.

The knight was not in a receptive mood, and he didn't want to listen to a pigeon's philosophy. For a moment he considered plunging forward into the darkness of the castle and blundering his way through. The blackness, however, was quite forbidding and, without his sword, he was afraid. It seemed he had no choice but to figure out what the inscription meant. He sighed and sat down. He read the words again:

Have you mistaken need for love?

The knight knew he loved Juliet and Christopher, although he had to admit that he loved Juliet more before she began sticking her head under wine casks and emptying their contents into her mouth.

Sam said, "Yes, you *love* Juliet and Christopher, but don't you *need* them too?"

"I suppose so," granted the knight. He had needed all the beauty that Juliet brought to his life with her quick wit and lovely poetry. He had also needed the nice things she did, like preparing little snacks for him to take on his crusades.

He thought back to the times when the knight business had been slow and they couldn't afford to buy new clothes or to employ cooks and serving maids. Juliet had made attractive garments for the family to wear, and she had prepared delicious meals for the knight and his friends. Fondly, the knight recalled that she also kept a very clean castle—and he had given her a lot of castles to keep clean too. Often they had had to move into a cheaper one when he came home broke after a crusade. He had left Juliet on her own to do most of the moving, as he was usually off at some tournament. How weary she had looked as she hauled their belongings from castle to castle, and how sad she had become when she realized she was unable to reach him through his armor.

"Isn't that when Juliet started lying under wine casks?" asked Sam.

The knight nodded. Tears began to form in his eyes. Then a dreadful thought occurred to him: He hadn't wanted to blame himself for the things he had done. He preferred to blame Juliet for all her wine drinking. Indeed, he used that to justify that everything was her fault—including his being stuck in his armor.

As the knight realized how unfairly he had treated Juliet, tears flowed down his face. Yes, he needed her more than he loved her. He wished he could love her more and need her less, but he didn't know how. Soon it dawned on him that he needed Christopher, too, more than he loved him. A knight needed his son to go out and do battle in his father's name when the father grew old. This didn't mean the knight didn't love Christopher, for he adored his son's golden-haired beauty. He also felt happy when he heard Christopher say, "I love you, Father," but as he had loved these things about Christopher, they had answered a need in him as well.

In a blinding flash, a thought struck the knight: He needed the love of Juliet and Christopher because he didn't love himself! In fact, he needed the love of all the damsels he had rescued and all the people for whom he had fought in crusades because he didn't love himself.

The knight cried harder as he realized that if he didn't love himself, he really couldn't love others. His need for them would get in the way. As he admitted this, a beautiful, bright light blossomed around him where there once had been total darkness. A hand touched his shoulder gently. Looking up through his tears, he saw Merlin smiling down.

"You have discovered a great truth," the magician told the knight. "You can love others only to the extent that you love yourself."

"But how do I begin to love myself?" the knight asked, blinking away his tears.

"You already have just by knowing what you know."

"I know I'm a fool," sobbed the knight.

"No, you know truth, and truth is love."

Comforted, the knight stopped crying. As his eyes dried, he noticed the light around him. It was unlike any light he had ever seen before. It seemed to come from nowhere, yet everywhere.

Merlin echoed the knight's thought. "There is nothing more beautiful than the light of self-knowledge."

The knight peered past the light into the dark gloom beyond. "There's no darkness in this castle for you, is there?"

"No," Merlin replied. "Not anymore."

Encouraged, the knight got to his feet, ready to continue. He thanked Merlin for showing up even when he hadn't called him.

"That is all right," assured the magician. "One does not always know when to ask for help." And so saying, he vanished.

As the knight forged ahead, Rebecca came flying out of the darkness.

"Wow!" she said, all atwitter. "Do I have something to show you!"

The knight had never seen Rebecca so excited. She hopped up and down on his shoulder, scarcely able to contain herself as she guided the knight and Squirrel to a large mirror. "That's it! That's it!" she cried with delight, her eyes sparkling.

The knight was disappointed. "It's only a crummy old mirror. C'mon, let's get going."

"It's not an *ordinary* mirror," Rebecca insisted. "It doesn't show what you *look* like. It shows what you're *really* like."

The knight was intrigued but reluctant to look at himself. He had never cared much for mirrors because he had never considered himself handsome. But at Rebecca's urging he stood before the mirror and gazed at his reflection. To his amazement, instead of a tall man with sad eyes and a large nose, armored to the neck, he saw a charming, vital person whose eyes shone with compassion and love.

He frowned in puzzlement. "Who's that?"

"It's *you*," Squirrel answered.

The knight shook his head. "This mirror is a phony. I don't look like that."

"You're seeing the *real* you," explained Sam, "the you who lives beneath your armor."

"But," protested the knight, looking deeper into the mirror, "that man is a perfect specimen. And his face is full of beauty and innocence."

"That's your potential," Sam said. "To be beautiful and innocent and perfect."

"If that's my potential, something terrible happened on my way to it."

"Yes," Sam agreed. "You put an invisible armor between you and your real feelings. It's been there for such a long time that it's become visible and permanent."

"Maybe I did hide my feelings," admitted the knight. "But I couldn't just say everything I felt like saying and do everything I felt like doing. Nobody would have liked me."

He stopped short as he uttered these words, realizing he had lived his whole life in a way that he believed would make people like him. He thought of all the crusades he had fought in, all the dragons he had slain, and all the damsels he had rescued—all to prove he was good, kind, and loving. The truth was, he didn't have to prove anything. He *was* good, kind, and loving.

"Jumping javelins!" he exclaimed. "I've wasted my whole life!"

"No," Sam said quickly. "It hasn't been wasted. You've needed time to learn what you just learned."

"I still feel like crying."

"Now *that* would be a waste," said Sam. Then he sang this little tune:

"Tears of self-pity end up in disgust.

They're not the kind that cause armor to rust."

The knight was in no mood to appreciate Sam's singing or his humor. "Stop with the tiresome rhymes or you're outta here," he growled.

"You can't get rid of me," chortled Sam. "I'm *you*. Remember?"

At that point the knight gladly would have shot himself to shut Sam up, but fortunately guns hadn't been invented yet. It seemed he was stuck with him.

The knight looked into the mirror again. Kindness, love, compassion, intelligence, and unselfishness looked back at him. Then it dawned on him. The only thing he had to do to have these qualities was reclaim them, for they had been his all along.

At this thought, the beautiful light fanned out and grew brighter than before. It illuminated the whole room, revealing, to the knight's surprise, that the castle had only one gigantic room.

"It's the standard building code for a Castle of Knowledge," Sam explained. "Real knowledge isn't divided into compartments because it all stems from one truth."

The knight nodded proudly in agreement. Just as he was ready to leave, Squirrel came running up. "This castle has a courtyard with a big apple tree growing in the center of it!"

"Really? Take me to it, quickly!" said the knight eagerly, for he was getting quite hungry.

The knight and Rebecca followed Squirrel into the courtyard. The sturdy boughs of the huge tree bent under the weight of the reddest, shiniest apples the knight had ever seen.

"How do you like them apples?" quipped Sam.

The knight couldn't help but chuckle. Then he

noticed an inscription chiseled into a slab of stone beside the tree:

FOR THIS FRUIT, I IMPOSE NO CONDITION,
BUT MAY YOU NOW LEARN ABOUT AMBITION.

The knight pondered this but quite frankly had no idea what it meant. Shrugging, he decided to ignore it.

"If you do, we'll never get out of here," said Sam.

The knight groaned. "These inscriptions are getting harder and harder to understand."

"No one ever said the Castle of Knowledge would be a breeze."

The knight sighed, picked an apple, and sat down under the tree with Rebecca and Squirrel. He jerked his head toward the inscription. "Either of you get this one?" he asked.

Squirrel shook her head.

The knight looked at Rebecca, who also shook her head. "But I *do* know," she said thoughtfully, "that I don't have any ambition."

"Neither do I," chimed in Squirrel, "and I'll bet this tree doesn't have any either."

"She's on to something," Rebecca pointed out. "This tree is like us. It has no ambition. Maybe you don't need any."

"That's all right for trees and animals," said the knight. "But what would a person be without ambition?"

"Happy," Sam piped up.

"No, I don't think so."

"All of you are correct," said a familiar voice.

The knight turned and saw Merlin standing behind him and the animals. The magician was dressed in his long white robe. He was carrying a lute.

"I was about to call you," said the knight.

"I know," replied the magician. "Everyone needs help to understand a tree. Trees are content just being trees—the same as Rebecca and Squirrel are happy just being what they are."

"But human beings are different," protested the knight. "They have minds."

"We have minds too," declared Squirrel, somewhat offended.

"Sorry. It's just that human beings have very complicated minds that make them want to become better," explained the knight.

Merlin idly plucked a few notes on his lute. "Better than what?"

"Better than they *are*," answered the knight.

"Humans are born beautiful, innocent, and perfect. What could be better than that?" Merlin countered.

"No, I mean that they want to be better than they think they are, and they want to be better than others are. You know, like I've always wanted to be the best knight in the kingdom."

"Ah, yes," said Merlin, "ambition from that complicated mind of yours led you to try to prove that you were better than other knights."

"What's wrong with that?" the knight asked, growing defensive.

"How could you be better than other knights when they were all born as beautiful, innocent, and perfect as you were?"

"I was happy trying."

"Were you? Or were you so busy trying to become that you couldn't enjoy just *being*?"

"You're getting me all confused," muttered the knight. "I know people need ambition. They want to be smart and have nice castles and be able to trade in last year's horse for a new one. They want to get ahead."

"You are talking about people's desire to be rich, but if a person is kind, loving, compassionate, intelligent, and unselfish, how could that person be richer?"

"Well, those riches can't buy castles and horses," replied the knight, slightly annoyed.

Merlin smiled. "It is true that there is more than one kind of riches—just as there is more than one kind of ambition."

The knight shrugged. "Seems to me that ambition is ambition. Either you want to get ahead or you don't."

"There is more to it than that," explained the magician. "Ambition that comes from the mind can get you nice castles and fine horses. However, only ambition that comes from the heart can bring happiness."

"What's ambition from the heart?"

"Ambition from the heart is pure. It competes with no one and harms no one. In fact, it serves one in such a way that it serves others at the same time."

"How?"

"This is where we can learn from the apple tree," Merlin said, gesturing above him. "It has become handsome and fully mature, bearing fine fruit, which it gives freely to all. The more apples people pick, the more the tree grows and the more beautiful it becomes. This tree is doing exactly what apple trees are meant to do—fulfilling its potential to the benefit of all. The same applies to people when they have ambition from the heart."

"But," objected the knight, "if I sat around all day giving away free apples, I wouldn't own a classy castle and be able to trade in last year's horse for a new one."

"You, like most people, want to have lots of nice things, but it is necessary to separate need from greed."

"Tell that to a wife who wants a castle in a better neighborhood," retorted the knight with a grunt.

A look of amusement flickered across Merlin's face. "You could pick these apples and sell some of them to pay for a new castle and horse. Then you could give away the apples you do not need so that others could be nourished."

The knight sighed. "It's easier for trees than it is for people in this world," he said philosophically.

"It is all a matter of perception. You receive the same life energy as the tree. You use the same water, the same air, and the same nourishment from the earth. I assure you that if you learn from the tree, you too can bring forth the fruits that nature intended—and you will soon have all the horses and castles you could want. So what do you think?"

Scratching his head, the knight said, "You mean I could get everything I need just by having roots and staying in my own backyard?"

Merlin laughed. "Human beings were given two feet so they would not have to stay in one place, but if they would stand still more often to accept and appreciate instead of running around to grab, they would truly understand ambition from the heart."

The knight sat quietly, contemplating Merlin's words. He studied the apple tree flourishing above him. He looked at Squirrel, then Rebecca, then Merlin. Neither the tree nor the animals had ambition, and Merlin's ambition was obviously from the heart. They all appeared happy and well nourished; all were beautiful specimens of life.

Then he examined himself—scrawny, nervous, and exhausted from lugging around his heavy armor. All this he had acquired by ambition from the mind, and all this he now knew he must change. The idea was

frightening, but then again, he had already lost everything, so what did he have to lose?

"From this moment on, my ambition will come
from the heart," he pledged.

As the knight spoke these words, both the castle
and Merlin disappeared, and the knight found himself
back on the Path of Truth with Rebecca and Squirrel.
Running alongside the path was a sparkling brook.
Thirsty, he knelt to drink from it. When he saw his
reflection in the water, he gasped. The armor that had
covered his arms and legs had rusted and fallen away,
and his beard was long once more. Evidently, the
Castle of Knowledge, like the Castle of Silence, had
played tricks with time. The knight contemplated this
rather odd phenomenon and soon realized Merlin had
been right. Time *does* pass quickly when one is listening to oneself. He recollected how often time had
dragged on and on when he was depending on others
to fill it.

With all his armor gone except for the breastplate,
the knight felt lighter and younger than he had in
years. He also found that he liked himself better than
he had in years.

Pressing forward with the brisk step of a young
man, he started out for the Castle of Will and Daring,
Rebecca flying above him and Squirrel scrambling at
his heels.

Chapter Six

The Castle of Will and Daring

*B*y dawn the next day, the unlikely trio came to the final castle. It was taller than the first two and its walls looked thicker. Confident he would be able to pass through this castle as well, the knight immediately started across the drawbridge.

When they were halfway across, the door to the castle flew open and out lumbered a huge, menacing, fire-breathing dragon with shiny green scales.

Shocked, the knight stopped dead in his tracks. He had seen some dragons in his time, but this one beat them all. It was enormous, and flames roared not only out of its mouth—as was the case with any run-of-the-mill dragon—but also out of its eyes and ears. To make matters worse, the flames were blue. This dragon had a high butane content.

The knight automatically reached for his sword, but his hand fell away empty. He began to tremble. In a croaky, unrecognizable voice, the knight called out to Merlin for help, but much to his dismay, the magician didn't appear.

"What's happening? Why won't he come?" the knight uttered in a panicky voice as he dodged a jet of blue flame from the monster.

"I don't know," said Squirrel. "He's usually pretty reliable."

Rebecca flew onto the knight's shoulder, cocked her head, and listened attentively. "From what I can pick up, Merlin's in Paris attending a magicians' conference."

A flurry of thoughts ran through the knight's head. *He can't let me down now! He promised there wouldn't be any dragons on the Path of Truth!*

"He meant ordinary dragons," roared the monster in a booming voice that shook the trees and nearly knocked Rebecca off the knight's shoulder.

The situation was grave. A dragon that could read minds was absolutely the worst kind. Somehow, some way, the knight forced himself to stop trembling. Summoning his strongest, loudest voice, he shouted, "Get out of my way, you oversized Bunsen burner bully!"

The beast snorted, sending fire in all directions. "Tough talk from a scaredy-cat."

Not knowing what to do next, the knight stalled for time. "What are you doing in the Castle of Will and Daring?"

"Why, I'm the Dragon of Fear and Doubt. Can you think of a better place for me to live?"

The knight had to admit this dragon was well named. Fear and doubt were precisely what he was feeling at the moment.

The dragon raised its head high. "I'm here to knock off all you smart alecks who think you can lick anybody just because you've been through the Castle of Knowledge."

Rebecca whispered in the knight's ear. "Merlin once said that self-knowledge can kill the Dragon of Fear and Doubt."

"Do you believe that?" the knight whispered back.

"Yes."

"Then *you* take on that jolly green flame thrower!" he cried, pushing her off his shoulder. Then he whirled and quickly retreated across the drawbridge.

"Ho, ho, ho!" bellowed the dragon triumphantly, the last "ho" nearly igniting the seat of the knight's pants.

"Are you quitting after you've come this far?" Squirrel called out as the knight brushed sparks from his backside.

"I don't know," the knight shot back, huffing and puffing. "I've become used to some little luxuries — like *living*!"

Sam chimed in. "How can you live with yourself if you don't have the will and daring to test your self-knowledge?"

The knight rolled his eyes. "Not you again. So you

believe it too? You think that self-knowledge can kill this dragon?"

"Certainly. Self-knowledge is truth, and you know what they say: Truth is mightier than the sword."

"I *know* they say that, but has anybody ever proved it and lived?" quibbled the knight.

As soon as he uttered these words, the knight remembered he didn't need to prove anything. He was born good, kind, and loving. Therefore, he didn't have to feel fear and doubt. The dragon was only an illusion.

He screeched to a halt so abruptly that Squirrel, who was right behind, almost ran into him. Turning, the knight looked back across the drawbridge. The monster was pawing the ground and setting fire lazily to some nearby bushes, apparently to keep in practice. Realizing the dragon existed only if he believed it did, the knight took a deep breath and slowly marched back over the drawbridge.

The dragon, of course, came out to meet the knight again, snorting and spitting fire. This time, however, the knight continued marching forward. His courage soon began to melt, as did his beard, from the intense heat of the dragon's flame. With a cry of fear and anguish, he turned once again and ran.

Letting out a mighty laugh, the dragon shot a stream of searing flame at the retreating knight. With a howl of pain, the knight fled across the drawbridge with Squirrel and Rebecca close behind him. Spotting a small brook, he quickly plunged his scorched seat into the cool water, quenching the flames with a hiss.

Squirrel and Rebecca stood on the bank trying to comfort him.

"You were very brave," said Squirrel.

"Not bad for a first try," added Rebecca.

Astonished, the knight looked up from where he sat. "What do you mean, *first* try?"

Squirrel said matter-of-factly, "You'll do better when you go back the second time."

The knight shook a finger angrily at his furry companion. "*You* go back a second time!"

"Remember, the dragon was only an illusion," said Rebecca.

"And the fire coming out of its mouth? Was that an illusion too?"

"Right," the pigeon replied. "That was an illusion too."

"Then why am I sitting in this brook with a burned behind?" demanded the knight.

"Because you made the fire real by believing that the dragon is real," explained Rebecca.

"If you believe the Dragon of Fear and Doubt is real, you give it the power to burn your behind—or anything else," said Squirrel.

"They're right," added Sam. "You have to go back and face the dragon once and for all."

The knight felt cornered. It was three against one. Or rather, it was two and a half against a half; for the Sam half of the knight agreed with Squirrel and Rebecca, while the other half wanted to stay in the brook.

As the knight grappled with his flagging courage, he heard Sam say, "God gave man courage. Courage gives God to man."

The knight was flustered, angry, and embarrassed. "I'm tired of figuring out what things mean. I'd much rather just sit here and forget about it."

"Look," Sam said encouragingly, "if you *face* the dragon, there's a *chance* it will destroy you, but if you *don't* face the dragon, it will *surely* destroy you."

"Decisions are simple when there's no alternative," snapped the knight. Reluctantly he struggled to his feet, took a deep breath, and once again started across the drawbridge.

The dragon looked up in disbelief. This was certainly a stubborn fellow. "Back again?" it snorted. "Well, *this* time I'm *really* going to make you burn!"

But a different knight was marching toward the dragon now—a knight who chanted over and over, "Fear and doubt are illusions. Fear and doubt are illusions."

The dragon hurled gigantic, crackling flames at the knight again and again, but its fire bolts had no effect. As the knight continued to approach, the dragon became smaller and smaller until it was finally no bigger than a frog. Its flame extinguished, it began to spit small seeds at the knight. But these seeds—the Seeds of Doubt—didn't stop the knight either. The dragon grew even smaller. The knight raised his arms in triumph.

"I've won!" he shouted.

In a tiny voice, the dragon hissed, "Perhaps this time, but I'll be back again and again to stand in your way." With that, it vanished in a puff of blue smoke.

"Come back whenever you want," the knight called after it mockingly. "Each time you do, I'll be stronger and you'll be weaker."

Rebecca landed on the knight's shoulder. "You see? I was right. Self-knowledge *can* defeat the Dragon of Fear and Doubt."

"If you truly believed that, why didn't you march up to the dragon with me?" asked the knight, no longer feeling inferior to his feathered friend.

Rebecca fluffed her feathers. "I didn't want to interfere. It's your trip."

Amused, the knight continued toward the Castle of Will and Daring. When he reached the entrance, the castle suddenly disappeared.

Sam explained, "You don't have to learn will and daring, because you've just shown that you already have them."

The knight threw back his head and laughed with

pure joy. Looking ahead, he could see the top of the mountain. The path appeared to be much steeper than it had been, but it didn't matter.

Nothing could stop him now.

CHAPTER SEVEN

The Summit of Truth

Inch by inch, hand over hand, the knight climbed, his fingers cut and bleeding from the sharp rocks. When he was almost to the top, his path was blocked by a huge boulder. Not surprisingly, it had an inscription on it:

THOUGH THIS UNIVERSE I OWN,

I POSSESS NOT A THING,

FOR I CANNOT KNOW THE UNKNOWN

IF TO THE KNOWN I CLING.

The knight was too exhausted to overcome this final hurdle. How was he to decipher the inscription while clinging to the side of the mountain? It seemed impossible, but he knew he had to try. Squirrel and Rebecca were tempted to offer their sympathy; however, they knew that sympathy can weaken a human being.

The knight took a deep breath, which helped clear his head. Then he read the last two lines of the inscription aloud: "for I cannot know the unknown if to the known I cling."

He considered some of the knowns to which he had been clinging all his life. There was his identity—who he thought he was and who he thought he wasn't. There were his beliefs—those things he thought were true and those he thought were false. And there were his judgments—the things he held as good and those he held as bad.

The knight looked up at the boulder, and a horrifying thought entered his mind: The rock to which he was clinging for dear life was also known to him. Would he have to let go and fall into the abyss of the unknown?

"You've figured it out, Knight," said Sam. "You have to let go."

The knight's eyes grew wide with alarm. "What are you trying to do? Kill both of us?" he yelled at Sam.

"Actually, we're dying right now," Sam answered calmly. "Take a look at yourself. You're so thin you could slip under a door, and you're full of stress and fear."

"I'm not *nearly* as afraid as I used to be."

"If that's the case, then let go—and *trust*."

"Trust *whom*?" the knight retorted hotly. He wanted no more of Sam's philosophy.

"It's not a *whom*," Sam replied. "It's an *it*!"

"*It?*"

"Yes, *It*—life, the force, the universe, God—whatever you want to call it."

The knight peered over his shoulder and looked down at the apparently bottomless chasm below.

"Let go," Sam whispered urgently.

The knight seemed to have no choice. He was losing strength with every passing second, and the cuts on his fingers were getting deeper the longer he hung onto the rock. Believing that he was going to die, he let go. Down, down he plunged, into the infinite depth of his memories.

He recalled all the things in his life for which he had blamed his mother, his father, his teachers, his wife, his son, his friends, and everyone else. As he fell deeper into the void, he let go of all the judgments that he had made against them.

Faster and faster he plummeted, giddy as his mind descended into his heart. Then, for the first time, he saw his life clearly, without judgment or excuses. In that instant, he accepted full responsibility for his life, for the influence that people had had on it, and for the events that had shaped it.

From this moment on, he would no longer blame his mistakes and misfortunes on anyone or anything outside himself. The recognition that he was the cause, not the effect, gave him a new feeling of power. He was now unafraid.

As an unfamiliar sense of calm overtook him, a strange thing happened. He began to fall *upward*! Impossible as it seemed, he was falling up, up, out of the abyss! At the same time, he still felt connected to the deepest part of it. In fact, he felt connected to the very center of the earth. He continued falling higher and higher, knowing that he was joined with both heaven and earth.

Suddenly he found himself standing on top of the mountain. Smiling, the knight understood the full meaning of the inscription on the boulder. He had let go of all that he had feared and all that he had known and possessed. His willingness to embrace the unknown had set him free. Now the universe was his to experience and enjoy.

The knight stood on the mountaintop, breathing deeply. An overwhelming sense of well-being swept through him. He grew dizzy from the enchantment of seeing, hearing, and feeling the universe all around him. Before, fear of the unknown had dulled his senses, but now he was able to experience everything with breathtaking clarity. The warmth of the afternoon sun, the melody of the gentle mountain breeze, and the beauty of nature's shapes and colors that painted the landscape as far as his eyes could see filled him with indescribable pleasure. His heart overflowed with love—for himself, for Juliet and Christopher, for Merlin, for Squirrel and Rebecca, for life itself, and for the entire wondrous world.

Squirrel and Rebecca watched the knight drop to his knees, tears of gratitude flowing from his eyes. *I nearly died from the tears I left unshed,* he thought. The tears poured down his cheeks, through his beard, and onto his breastplate. Because they came from his heart, the tears were extraordinarily hot and quickly melted away the last of his armor.

The knight cried out with joy. No longer would he don his armor and ride off in all directions. No longer would people see the shining reflection of steel and think that the sun was rising in the west or setting in the east.

He smiled through his tears, unaware that a radiant new light now shone from him—a light far brighter and more beautiful than his armor at its polished best—sparkling like a brook, glowing like the moon, dazzling like the sun.

For indeed, the knight *was* the brook. He *was* the moon. He *was* the sun. He could be all these things and more, because he was one with the universe.

He was love.

The Beginning

*Treat Yourself to This Fun, Inspirational Book
and Discover How to Find Happiness and Serenity . . .
No Matter What Life Dishes Out*

The Dragon Slayer
With a Heavy Heart

**This powerful story by bestselling author Marcia Grad Powers
promises to be one of the most important you will ever read—
and one of the most memorable.**

Sometimes things happen we wish hadn't. Sometimes things don't happen we wish would. We might wish our past had been different or that *we* could be different. We struggle through disappointments... frustrations...losses...and more. We do the best we can and hope things get better. In the meantime, our hearts can grow heavy.

That's what happened to Duke the Dragon Slayer. In fact, his heart grew *so* heavy with all that he felt was unfair and not the way it should be, he became desperate to lighten it—and set forth on the Path of Serenity to find out how.

Guided by fascinating characters that spring to life and become his personal friends, Duke finds out the secret to being okay even when things aren't okay.

Accompany Duke on this life-changing adventure. His guides will be your guides. His tools will be your tools. His success will be your success. And by the time he is heading home, both Duke and you will know how to take life's inevitable lumps and bumps in stride—and find happiness and serenity anytime . . . even when you really, REALLY wish some things were different.

"A BEAUTIFUL, EXCEPTIONALLY WELL-WRITTEN STORY THAT WILL BE OF INVALUABLE HELP TO EVERYONE..."

Albert Ellis, Ph.D., President
Albert Ellis Institute
Author of *A Guide to Rational Living*

I invite you to meet an extraordinary princess and accompany her on an enlightening journey. You will laugh with her and cry with her, learn with her and grow with her . . . and she will become a dear friend you will never forget.

Marcia Grad Powers

1 MILLION COPIES SOLD WORLDWIDE

The Princess Who Believed in Fairy Tales

"Here is a very special book that will guide you lovingly into a new way of thinking about yourself and your life so that the future will be filled with hope and love and song."

OG MANDINO
Author, *The Greatest Salesman in the World*

The Princess Who Believed in Fairy Tales by Marcia Grad is a personal growth book of the rarest kind. It's a delightful, humor-filled story you will experience so deeply that it can literally change your feelings about yourself, your relationships, and your life.

The princess's journey of self-discovery on the Path of Truth is an eye-opening, inspiring, empowering psychological and spiritual journey that symbolizes the one we all take through life as we separate illusion from reality, come to terms with our childhood dreams and pain, and discover who we really are and how life works.

If you have struggled with childhood pain, with feelings of not being good enough, with the loss of your dreams, or if you have been disappointed in your relationships, this book will prove to you that happy endings—and new beginnings—are always possible. Or, if you simply wish to get closer to your own truth, the princess will guide you.

The universal appeal of this book has resulted in its translation into numerous languages.

Excerpts from Readers' Heartfelt Letters

"*The Princess* is truly a gem! Though I've read a zillion self-help and spiritual books, I got more out of this one than from any other one I've ever read. It is just too illuminating and full of wisdom to ever be able to thank you enough. The friends and family I've given copies to have raved about it."

"*The Princess* is powerful, insightful, and beautifully written. I am seventy years old and have seldom encountered greater wisdom. I've been waiting to read this book my entire life. You are a psychologist, a guru, a saint, and an angel all wrapped up into one. I thank you with all my heart."

Available wherever books are sold or from **Wilshire Book Company**.
For our complete catalog or to order online, please visit **www.mpowers.com**